The Tomato Thief

Niyatee Parikh Sharma
Illustrated by Alankrita Amaya

tota books
An imprint of Speaking Tiger Books

Veer was eager to taste the tomatoes growing in the green patch in the terrace garden! He had been waiting for them to be ripe enough to eat!

"Can we pick them now, Mummy?"
"Be patient," she replied. "You have to
let them turn fully red before you pick them."

"How many days to go?" squealed Veer.
"Maybe three or four more days"

Veer waited with excitement...

Day 1

Day 2
Day 3

On the fourth day, something strange happened. When Veer went up to the terrace garden, he was shocked.

"Mummy, did you pick the ripe tomatoes?" he asked.

"No sweetheart, I did not touch them," exclaimed Mummy.

"But the red tomatoes are missing! Can they run away? Did someone steal them?"

"That's strange...who would steal tomatoes?" wondered Mummy.

"Could it be Baba?"

"NO," said Baba. "I knew you wanted to pick the tomatoes yourself. I did not touch them."

"Could it be Shobha Aunty, our cook?"

"No, Veer ammu, there were tomatoes in the fridge already. I did not go to the terrace yesterday. I did not touch them".

"Could it be naughty Ananya?" asked Veer.

"Your baby sister does love squashing tomatoes, but she couldn't have reached up so high. I'm sure she didn't touch them," reassured Mummy.

"Hmmmm...could it be Ramu Kaka, our maali?" thought Veer.

"Oh, no, Veer baba...never...I know how much you wanted to pluck them your-self! I did not touch them!"

"Who could it be then? Could it be my friends Pranav or Shreya?

"No Veer," said Pranav "I did not touch them."

"Nope" said Shreya. "When we played the hide-the-dinosaur game in your garden yesterday, I don't remember seeing any red tomatoes. I did not touch them."

"Just who could it be?" wondered Veer. "Did a spaceship land from the sky and steal my tomatoes?"

"Why don't you keep a watch tomorrow," suggested Mummy helpfully.

The next morning Veer noticed newly ripened tomatoes in the garden. He hid behind the pots for a long time to keep a watch.

Baba came outside to read the newspaper on the garden swing.

Shobha Aunty came to take a few curry leaves from the curry plant.

Naughty Ananya came and made a big muddy puddle on the terrace, jumped in it for a while and went away.

Ramu Kaka came to water the plants.

Shreya and Pranav came looking for Veer and went back. The red tomatoes were still there!

Suddenly there was a loud thadaaaaaam on the terrace.

First Veer spotted a long tail...
then big black paws...two pointy ears...
sharp teeth and a big black face!

It was a **MONKEY**
busy chomping away
a Red Juicy Tomato!

Veer came out of his hiding place. The monkey looked at Veer. Veer looked at the monkey.

Veer screamed loudly.
The monkey dashed away to a big tree nearby.
Veer quickly plucked the remaining red tomatoes before another tomato thief came by!

He took a big bite of the juicy vegetable...
Oh! How delicious it was!